HIPPO goes BANANAS!

by Marjorie Dennis Murray

illustrated by Kevin O'Malley

MARSHALL CAVENDISH CHILDREN

First Marshall Cavendish paperback edition, 2011

Marshall Cavendish Corporation, 99 White Plains Road, Tarrytown, NY 10591
www.marshallcavendish.us/kids

LIBRARY OF CONGRESS CATALOGING-IN-PUBLICATION DATA
Murray, Marjorie Dennis.
Hippo goes bananas! / by Marjorie Dennis Murray ; illustrated by Kevin O'Malley
p. cm.
Summary: As animals tell one another about Hippo's strange behavior, each makes up something terrible to add to the story, until they are frightened that Hippo will destroy the Serengeti itself.
978-0-7614-5224-9 (hardcover) 978-0-7614-5838-8 (paperback)
[1. Communication—Fiction. 2. Jungle animals—Fiction. 3. Toothache—Fiction. 4. Serengeti Plain (Tanzania)—Fiction. 5. Tanzania—Fiction. 6. Humorous stories.]
I. O'Malley, Kevin, 1961- ill. II. Title.
PZ7.M9635Hi 2005 [E]—dc22 2005009718

The illustrations are rendered in marker and colored pencil.
Book design by Michael Nelson

Printed in Malaysia (T)
1 3 5 6 4 2

With love, to my sister, Jill, who understands everything—even computers
—M. D. M.

Early one morning,
Hippo woke up
with a toothache.
"OOOOOOOO,
OOOOOOOO,
OOOOOOOO,"
he moaned.

He grumped and bellowed—
spun in circles—
and crashed into a tree.

He made so much noise that he woke up Cuckoo Bird.

Something's wrong with Hippo! thought Cuckoo Bird. *He's going bananas!* And off she flew to tell Monkey.

"Hippo's gone bananas!" said Cuckoo Bird. "He's knocking down every tree in the jungle!"

"Every tree in the jungle!" exclaimed Monkey.

"Yes, indeed!" said Cuckoo Bird. "And . . . and . . . kicking them off the cliff!"

"Great Gibbons!" said Monkey, and off he scampered to tell Leopard.

"Hippo's gone bananas!" said Monkey. "He's knocking down every tree in the jungle and kicking them off the cliff!"

"Kicking them off the cliff!" exclaimed Leopard.

"Yes, indeed!" said Monkey. "And . . . and . . . rolling them into the river!"

"Leaping Lemurs!" said Leopard, and off he dashed to tell Giraffe.

"Hippo's gone bananas!" said Leopard. "He's knocking down every tree in the jungle, kicking them off the cliff, and rolling them into the river!"

"Rolling them into the river!" exclaimed Giraffe.

"Yes, indeed!" said Leopard. "And . . . and . . . damming up the water!"

"Jumping Jackrabbits!" said Giraffe, and off she galloped to tell Zebra.

"Hippo's gone bananas!" said Giraffe. "He's knocking down every tree in the jungle, kicking them off the cliff, rolling them into the river, and damming up the water!"

"Damming up the water!" exclaimed Zebra.

"Yes, indeed!" said Giraffe. "And . . . and . . . flooding the Serengeti!"
"Wild Wildebeests!" said Zebra, and off she went to tell Elephant.

"Hippo's gone bananas!" said Zebra. "He's knocking down every tree in the jungle, kicking them off the cliff, rolling them into the river, damming up the water, and flooding the Serengeti!"

"Creeping Crocodiles!" exclaimed Elephant. "We've got to stop him!"

So off went all the animals to find Hippo.

In the hot, scorching sun Hippo groaned.
"OOOOOOOO, OOOOOOOO, OOOOOOOO."

He huffed and puffed in the sizzling heat—then he rolled on his back and kicked his feet.

Monkey scampered onto Hippo's snout.

"WHAT'S UP?" asked Monkey.

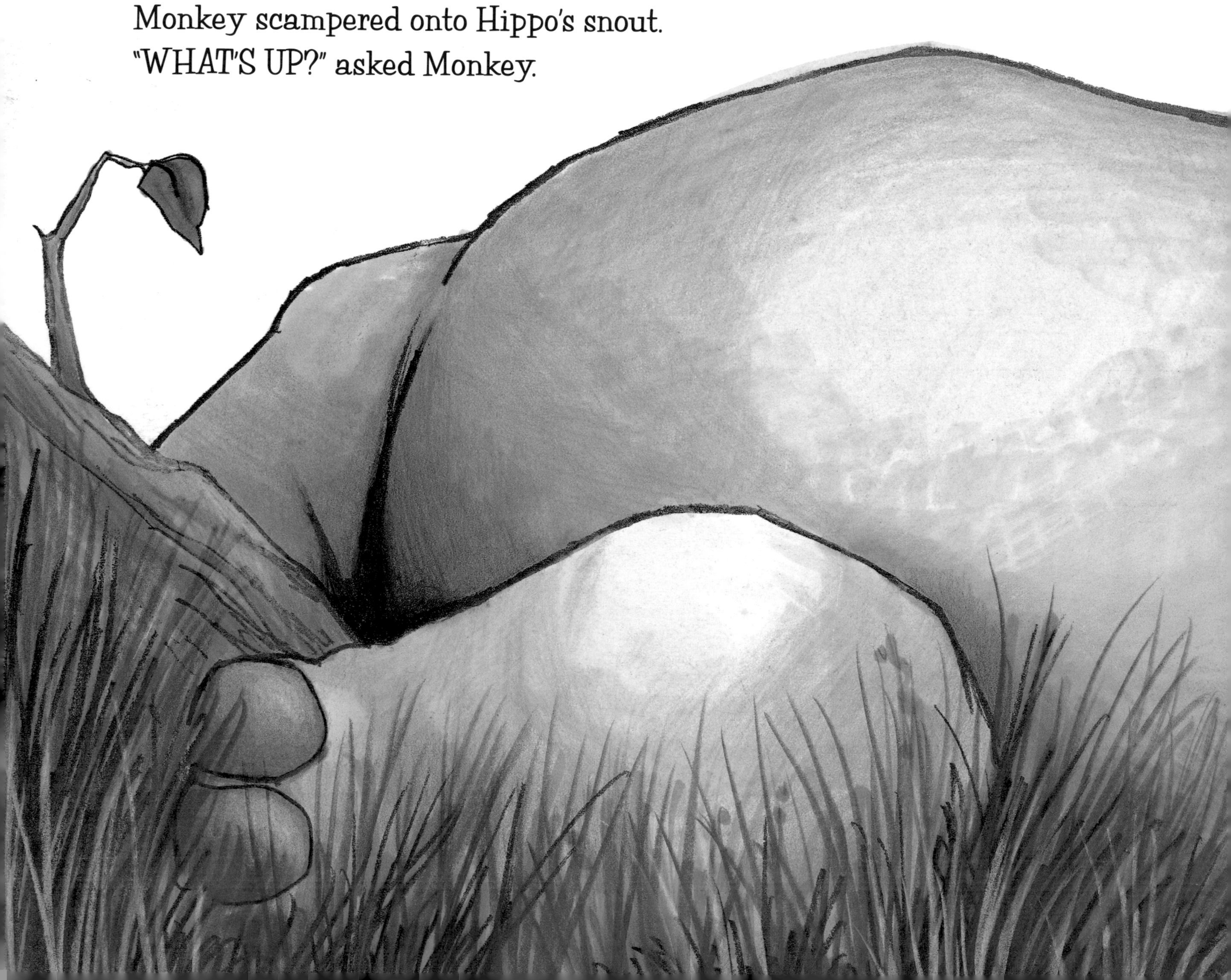

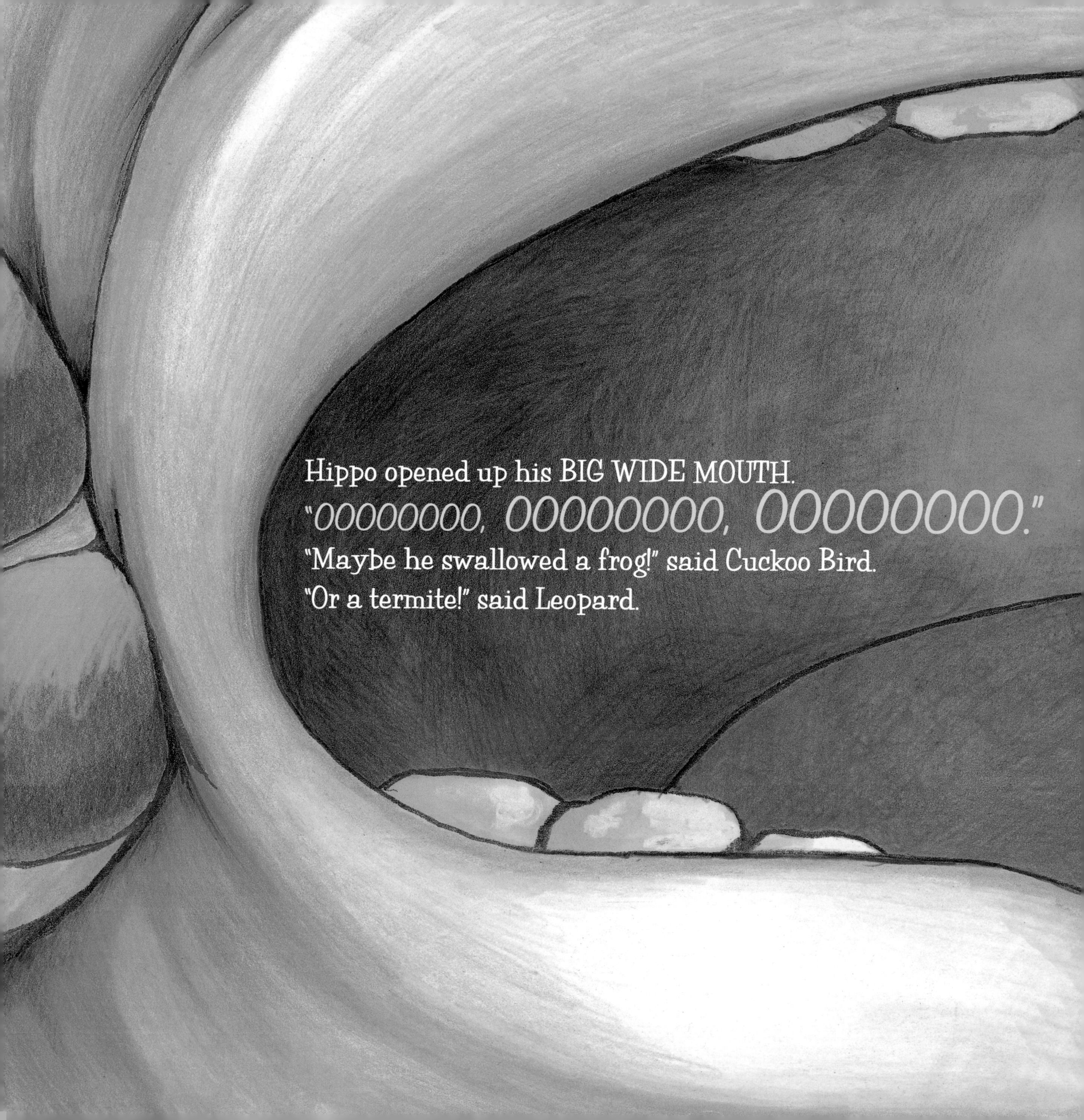

Hippo opened up his BIG WIDE MOUTH.

"OOOOOOOO, OOOOOOOO, OOOOOOOO."

"Maybe he swallowed a frog!" said Cuckoo Bird.

"Or a termite!" said Leopard.

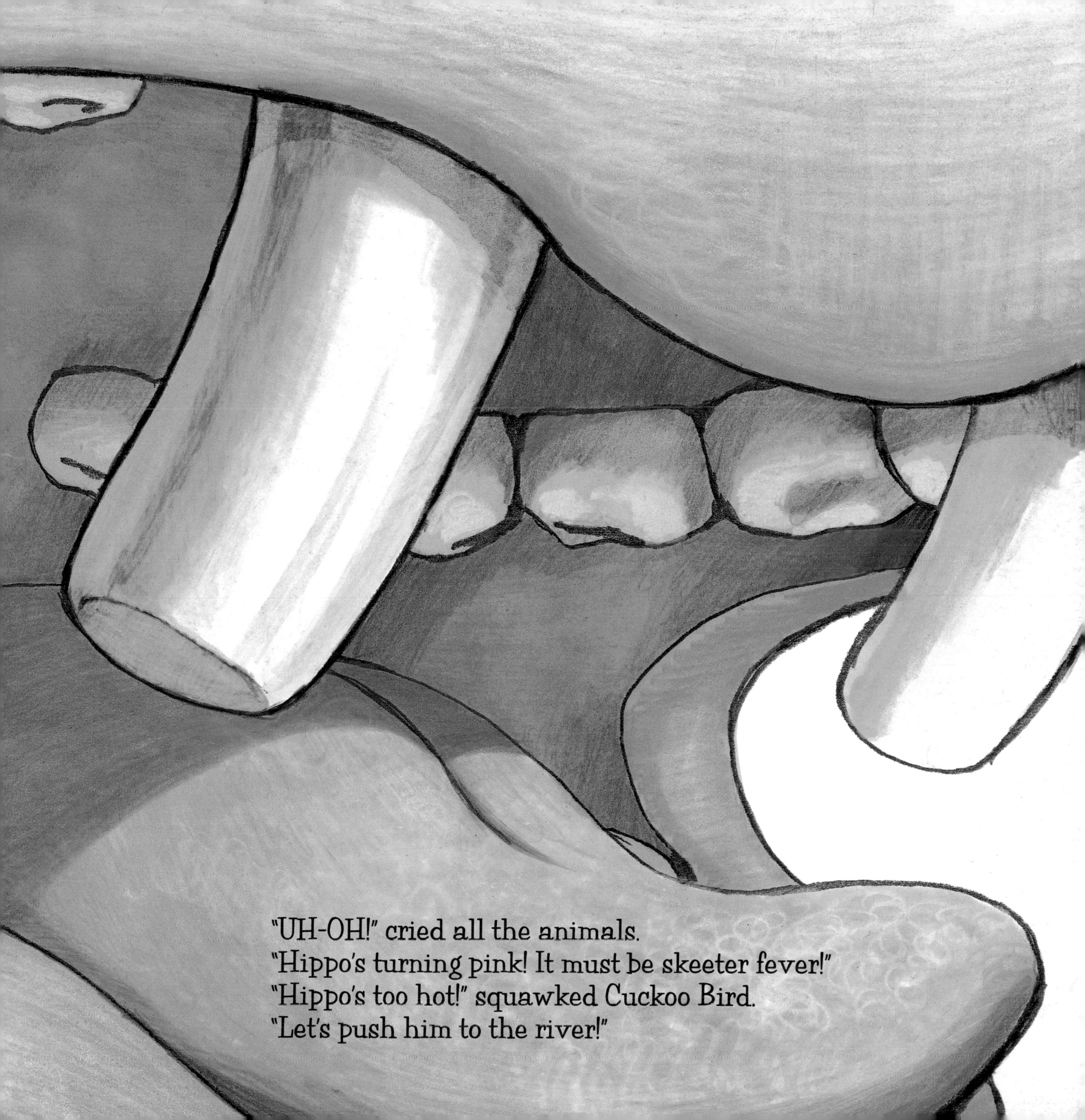

"UH-OH!" cried all the animals.
"Hippo's turning pink! It must be skeeter fever!"
"Hippo's too hot!" squawked Cuckoo Bird.
"Let's push him to the river!"

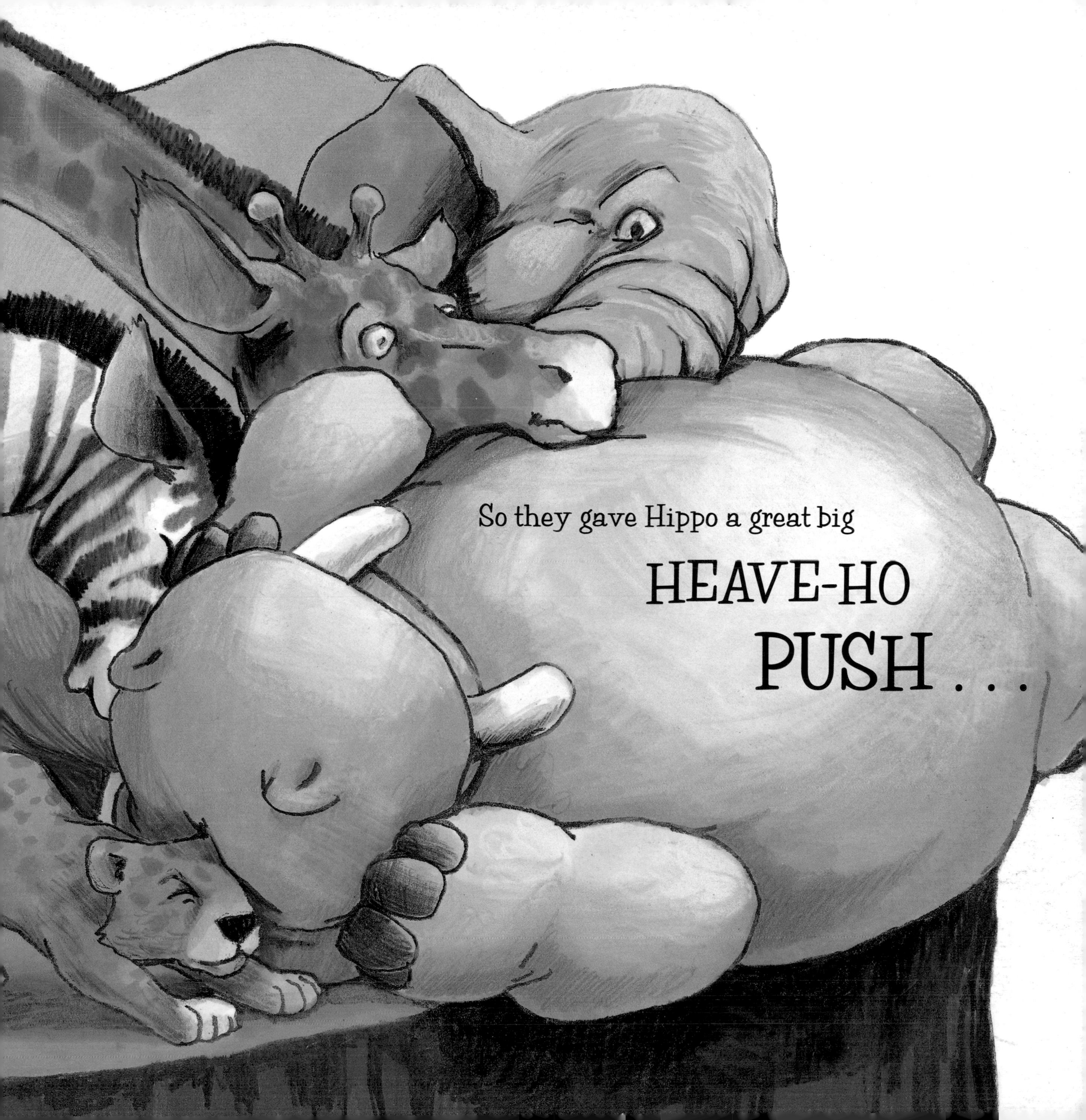

So they gave Hippo a great big

HEAVE-HO

PUSH . . .

. . . and off he bumped
down the mountainside,
rolling toward the river.

BUMPITY

BUMP!

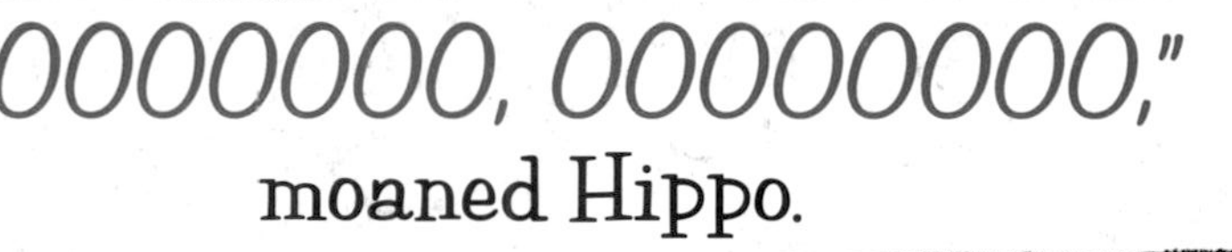
"OOOOOOOO, OOOOOOOO,"
moaned Hippo.

"OOOOOOOO, OOOOOOOO, OOOOOOOO."

And out came Hippo's tooth!

"OH!" exclaimed Cuckoo Bird.
"*That's* what was wrong with you!"

All the animals helped push Hippo onto his feet.

"Thank you," said Hippo. "MY TOOTHACHE IS GONE!

But now . . ."

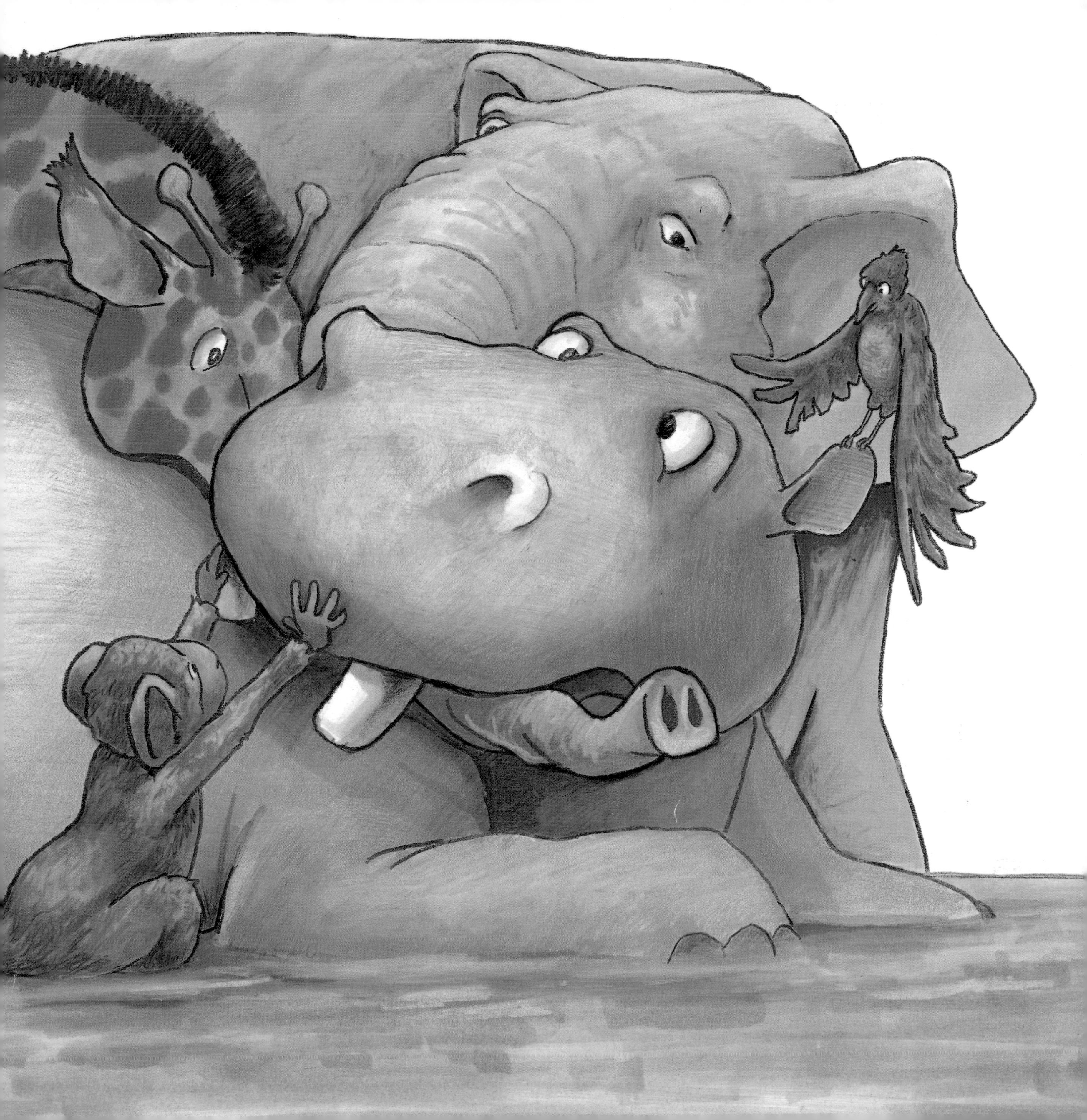

". . . MY **HEAD** ACHES!"